Rapunzel

Bilingual Edition: English – German
Zweisprachige Ausgabe: Englisch – Deutsch

Brothers Grimm
Brüder Grimm

ISBN-13: 9781521025185

Table of Contents
Inhaltsverzeichnis

Rapunzel

There were once a man and a woman who had long in vain wished for a child. At length the woman hoped that God was about to grant her desire. These people had a little window at the back of their house from which a splendid garden could be seen, which was full of the most beautiful flowers and herbs. It was, however, surrounded by a high wall, and no one dared to go into it because it belonged to an enchantress, who had great power and was dreaded by all the world. One day the woman was standing by this window and looking down into the garden, when she saw a bed which was planted with the most beautiful rampion (rapunzel), and it looked so fresh and green that she longed for it, and had the greatest desire to eat some. This desire increased every day, and as she knew that she could not get any of it, she quite pined away, and looked pale and miserable. Then her husband was alarmed, and asked, "What aileth thee, dear wife?" "Ah," she replied, "if I can't get some of the rampion, which is in the garden behind our house, to eat, I shall die." The man, who loved her, thought, "Sooner than let thy wife die, bring her some of the rampion thyself, let it cost thee what it will." In the twilight of evening, he clambered down over the wall into the garden of the enchantress, hastily clutched a handful of rampion, and took it to his wife. She at once made herself a salad of it, and ate it with much relish. She, however, liked it so much—so very much, that the next day she longed for it three times as much as before. If he was to have any rest, her husband must once more descend into the garden. In the gloom of evening, therefore, he let himself down again; but when he had clambered down the wall he was terribly afraid, for he saw the enchantress standing before him. "How canst thou dare," said she with angry look, "to descend into my garden and steal my rampion like a thief? Thou shalt suffer for it!" "Ah," answered he, "let mercy take the place of justice, I only made up my mind to do it out of necessity. My wife saw your rampion from the window, and felt such a longing for it that she would have died if she had not got some to eat." Then the enchantress allowed her anger to be softened, and said to him, "If the case be as thou sayest, I will allow thee to take away with thee as much rampion as thou wilt, only I make one condition, thou must give me the child which thy wife will bring into the world; it shall be well treated, and I will care for it like a mother." The man in his terror consented to everything, and when the woman was brought to bed, the enchantress appeared at once, gave the child the name of Rapunzel, and took it away with her.

Rapunzel grew into the most beautiful child beneath the sun. When she was twelve years old, the enchantress shut her into a tower, which lay in a forest, and had neither stairs nor door, but quite at the top was a little window. When the enchantress wanted to go in, she placed herself beneath this, and cried,

"Rapunzel, Rapunzel,
Let down thy hair to me."

Rapunzel had magnificent long hair, fine as spun gold, and when she heard the voice of the enchantress she unfastened her braided tresses, wound them round one of the hooks of the window above, and then the hair fell twenty ells down, and the enchantress climbed up by it.

After a year or two, it came to pass that the King's son rode through the forest and went by the tower. Then he heard a song, which was so charming that he stood still and listened. This was Rapunzel, who in her solitude passed her time in letting her sweet voice resound. The King's son wanted to climb up to her, and looked for the door of the tower, but none was to be found. He rode home, but the singing had so deeply touched his heart, that every day he went out into the forest and listened to it. Once when he was thus standing behind a tree, he saw that an enchantress came there, and he heard how she cried,

"Rapunzel, Rapunzel,
Let down thy hair."

Then Rapunzel let down the braids of her hair, and the enchantress climbed up to her. "If that is the ladder by which one mounts, I will for once try my fortune," said he, and the next day when it began to grow dark, he went to the tower and cried,

"Rapunzel, Rapunzel,
Let down thy hair."

Immediately the hair fell down and the King's son climbed up.

At first Rapunzel was terribly frightened when a man such as her eyes had never yet beheld, came to her; but the King's son began to talk to her quite like a friend, and told her that his heart had been so stirred that it had let him have no rest, and he had been forced to see her. Then Rapunzel lost her fear, and when he asked her if she would take him for her husband, and she saw that he was young and handsome, she thought, "He will love me more than old Dame Gothel does;" and she said yes, and laid her hand in his. She said, "I will willingly go away with thee, but I do not know how to get down. Bring with thee a skein of silk every time that thou comest, and I will weave a ladder with it, and when that is ready I will descend, and thou wilt take me on thy horse." They agreed that until that time he should come to her every evening, for the old woman came by day. The enchantress remarked nothing of this, until once Rapunzel said to her, "Tell me, Dame Gothel, how it happens that you are so much heavier for me to draw up than the young King's son—he is with me in a moment." "Ah! thou wicked child," cried the enchantress, "What do I hear thee say! I thought I had separated thee from all the world, and yet thou hast deceived me!" In her anger she clutched Rapunzel's beautiful tresses, wrapped them twice round her left hand, seized a pair of scissors with the right, and snip, snap, they were cut off, and the lovely braids lay on the ground. And she was so pitiless that she took poor Rapunzel into a desert where she had to live in great grief and misery.

On the same day, however, that she cast out Rapunzel, the enchantress in the evening fastened the braids of hair which she had cut off to the hook of the window, and when the King's son came and cried,

"Rapunzel, Rapunzel,
Let down thy hair,"

she let the hair down. The King's son ascended, but he did not find his dearest Rapunzel above, but the enchantress, who gazed at him with wicked and venomous looks. "Aha!" she cried mockingly, "Thou wouldst fetch thy dearest, but the beautiful bird sits no longer singing in the nest; the cat has got it, and will scratch out thy eyes as well. Rapunzel is lost to thee; thou wilt never see her more." The King's son was beside himself with pain, and in his despair he leapt down from the tower. He escaped with his life, but the thorns into which he fell, pierced his eyes. Then he wandered quite blind about the forest, ate nothing but roots and berries, and did nothing but lament and weep over the loss of his dearest wife. Thus he roamed about in misery for some years, and at length came to the desert where Rapunzel, with the twins to which she had given birth, a boy and a girl, lived in wretchedness. He heard a voice, and it seemed so familiar to him that he went towards it, and when he approached, Rapunzel knew him and fell on his neck and wept. Two of her tears wetted his eyes and they grew clear again, and he could see with them as before. He led her to his kingdom where he was joyfully received, and they lived for a long time afterwards, happy and contented.

Rapunzel

Es war einmal ein Mann und eine Frau, die wünschten sich schon lange vergeblich ein Kind, endlich machte sich die Frau Hoffnung, der liebe Gott werde ihren Wunsch erfüllen. Die Leute hatten in ihrem Hinterhause ein kleines Fenster, daraus konnte man in einen prächtigen Garten sehen, der voll der schönsten Blumen und Kräuter stand; er war aber von einer hohen Mauer umgeben und niemand wagte hineinzugehen, weil er einer Zauberin gehörte, die große Macht hatte und von aller Welt gefürchtet ward. Eines Tages stand die Frau an diesem Fenster und sah in den Garten hinab, da erblickte sie ein Beet, das mit den schönsten Rapunzeln bepflanzt war: und sie sahen so frisch und grün aus, daß sie lüstern ward und das größte Verlangen empfand, von den Rapunzeln zu essen. Das Verlangen nahm jeden Tag zu, und da sie wußte, daß sie keine davon bekommen konnte, so fiel sie ganz ab, sah blaß und elend aus. Da erschrak der Mann und fragte: »Was fehlt dir, liebe Frau?« »Ach,« antwortete sie, »wenn ich keine Rapunzeln aus dem Garten hinter unserem Hause zu essen kriege, so sterbe ich.« Der Mann, der sie lieb hatte, dachte: »Ehe du deine Frau sterben läßt, holst du ihr von den Rapunzeln, es mag kosten was es will.« In der Abenddämmerung stieg er also über die Mauer in den Garten der Zauberin, stach in aller Eile eine Hand voll Rapunzeln und brachte sie seiner Frau. Sie machte sich sogleich Salat daraus und aß sie in voller Begierde auf. Sie hatten ihr aber so gut, so gut geschmeckt, daß sie den anderen Tag noch dreimal so viel Lust bekam. Sollte sie Ruhe haben, so mußte der Mann noch einmal in den Garten steigen. Er machte sich also in der Abenddämmerung wieder hinab, als er aber die Mauer hinabgeklettert war, erschrak er gewaltig, denn er sah die Zauberin vor sich stehen. »Wie kannst du es wagen,« sprach sie mit zornigem Blick, »in meinen Garten zu steigen und wie ein Dieb mir meine Rapunzeln zu stehlen? Das soll dir schlecht bekommen.« »Ach,« antwortete er, »laßt Gnade für Recht ergehen, ich habe mich nur aus Not dazu entschlossen: meine Frau hat Euere Rapunzeln aus dem Fenster erblickt, und empfindet ein so großes Gelüsten, daß sie sterben würde, wenn sie nicht davon zu essen bekäme.« Da ließ die Zauberin in ihrem Zorne nach und sprach zu ihm: »Verhält es sich so, wie du sagst, so will ich dir gestatten, Rapunzeln mitzunehmen, soviel du willst, allein ich mache eine Bedingung: du mußt mir das Kind geben, das deine Frau zur Welt bringen wird. Es soll ihm gut gehen, und ich will für es sorgen wie eine Mutter.« Der Mann sagte in der Angst alles zu, und als die Frau in Wochen kam, so erschien sogleich die Zauberin, gab dem Kinde den Namen *Rapunzel* und nahm es mit sich fort.

Rapunzel ward das schönste Kind unter der Sonne. Als es zwölf Jahre alt war, schloß es die Zauberin in einen Turm, der in einem Walde lag und weder Treppe noch Thür hatte, nur ganz oben war ein kleines Fensterchen. Wenn die Zauberin hinein wollte, so stellte sie sich unten hin und rief:

»Rapunzel, Rapunzel,
laß mir dein Haar herunter.«

Rapunzel hatte lange prächtige Haare, fein wie gesponnen Gold. Wenn sie nun die Stimme der Zauberin vernahm, so band sie ihre Zöpfe los, wickelte sie oben um einen Fensterhaken und dann fielen die Haare zwanzig Ellen tief herunter, und die Zauberin stieg daran hinauf.

Nach ein paar Jahren trug es sich zu, daß der Sohn des Königs durch den Wald ritt und an dem Turm vorüberkam. Da hörte er einen Gesang, der war so lieblich, daß er still hielt und horchte. Das war Rapunzel, die in ihrer Einsamkeit sich die Zeit damit vertrieb, ihre süße Stimme erschallen zu lassen. Der Königssohn wollte zu ihr hinaufsteigen und suchte nach einer Thür des Turmes, aber es war keine zu finden. Er ritt heim, doch der Gesang hatte ihm so sehr das Herz gerührt, daß er jeden Tag hinaus in den Wald ging und zuhörte. Als er einmal so hinter einem Baume stand, sah er, daß eine Zauberin herankam und hörte wie sie hinaufrief:

»Rapunzel, Rapunzel,
laß dein Haar herunter.«

Da ließ Rapunzel die Haarflechten herab und die Zauberin stieg zu ihr hinauf. »Ist das die Leiter, auf welcher man hinaufkommt, so will ich auch einmal mein Glück versuchen.« Und den folgenden Tag, als es anfing dunkel zu werden, ging er zu dem Turm und rief

»Rapunzel, Rapunzel,
laß dein Haar herunter.«

Alsbald fielen die Haare herab und der Königssohn stieg hinauf.

Anfangs erschrak Rapunzel gewaltig, als ein Mann zu ihr hereinkam, wie ihre Augen noch nie einen erblickt hatten, doch der Königssohn fing an ganz freundlich mit ihr zu reden und erzählte ihr, daß von ihrem Gesange sein Herz so sehr sei bewegt worden, daß es ihm keine Ruhe gelassen, und er sie selbst habe sehen müssen. Da verlor Rapunzel ihre Angst, und als er sie fragte, ob sie ihn zum Manne nehmen wollte, und sie sah, daß er jung und schön war, so dachte sie: »Der wird mich lieber haben als die alte Frau Gothel,« und sagte ja, und legte ihre Hand in seine Hand. Sie sprach: »Ich will gern mit dir gehen, aber ich weiß nicht wie ich herabkommen kann. Wenn du kommst, so bring jedesmal einen Strang Seide mit, daraus will ich eine Leiter flechten und wenn die fertig ist, so steige ich herunter und du nimmst mich auf dein Pferd.« Sie verabredeten, daß er bis dahin alle Abend zu ihr kommen sollte, denn bei Tage kam die Alte. Die Zauberin merkte auch nichts davon, bis einmal Rapunzel anfing und zu ihr sagte: »Sag sie mir doch, Frau Gothel, wie kommt es nur, sie wird mir viel schwerer heraufzuziehen als der junge Königssohn, der ist in einem Augenblick bei mir.« »Ach, du gottloses Kind,« rief die Zauberin, »was muß ich von dir hören, ich dachte, ich hätte dich von aller Welt geschieden, und du hast mich doch betrogen!« In ihrem Zorne packte sie die schönen Haare der Rapunzel, schlug sie ein paarmal um ihre linke Hand, griff eine Schere mit der rechten, und ritsch, ratsch waren sie abgeschnitten, und die schönen Flechten lagen auf der Erde. Und sie war so unbarmherzig, daß sie die arme Rapunzel in eine Wüstenei brachte, wo sie in großem Jammer und Elend leben mußte.

Denselben Tag aber, wo sie Rapunzel verstoßen hatte, machte abends die Zauberin die abgeschnittenen Flechten oben am Fensterhaken fest, und als der Königssohn kam und rief:

»Rapunzel, Rapunzel,
laß dein Haar herunter.«

so ließ sie die Haare hinab. Der Königssohn stieg hinauf, aber er fand oben nicht seine liebste Rapunzel, sondern die Zauberin, die ihn mit bösen und giftigen Blicken ansah. »Aha,« rief sie höhnisch, »du willst die Frau Liebste holen, aber der schöne Vogel sitzt nicht mehr im Nest und singt nicht mehr, die Katze hat ihn geholt und wird dir auch noch die Augen auskratzen. Für dich ist Rapunzel verloren, du wirst sie nie wieder erblicken.« Der Königssohn geriet außer sich vor Schmerzen, und in der Verzweiflung sprang er den Turm herab; das Leben brachte er davon, aber die Dornen, in die er fiel, zerstachen ihm die Augen. Da irrte er blind im Walde umher, aß nichts als Wurzeln und Beeren, und that nichts als jammern und weinen über den Verlust seiner liebsten Frau. So wanderte er einige Jahre im Elend umher und geriet endlich in die Wüstenei, wo Rapunzel mit den Zwillingen, die sie geboren hatte, einem Knaben und Mädchen, kümmerlich lebte. Er vernahm eine Stimme, und sie däuchte ihm so bekannt: da ging er darauf zu, und wie er herankam, erkannte ihn Rapunzel und fiel ihm um den Hals und weinte. Zwei von ihren Thränen aber benetzten seine Augen, da wurden sie wieder klar, und er konnte damit sehen wie sonst. Er führte sie in sein Reich, wo er mit Freude empfangen ward, und sie lebten noch lange glücklich und vergnügt.

RAPUNZEL

RAPUNZEL

Made in the USA
Las Vegas, NV
03 February 2025

17514334R00015